THE ALCHEMIST'S LEGACY

Aurora Thorne

GLOBAL
PUBLISHING
SOLUTIONS

THE ALCHEMIST'S LEGACY by Aurora Thorne
Published by Global Publishing Solutions, LLC
923 Fieldside Drive
Matteson, Illinois 60443
www.globalpublishingsolutions.com

This book or parts thereof may not be reproduced in any form, stored in a retrieval system, or transmitted in any form by any means—electronic, mechanical, photocopy, recording, or otherwise—without prior permission of the publisher, except as provided by United States of America copyright law.

Copyright © 2024 by Aurora Thorne

All rights reserved.

International Standard Book Number:
9798330294244
E-book International Standard Book Number:
9798330294251

Unless otherwise indicated, all the names, characters, businesses, places, events, and incidents in this book are either the product of the author's imagination or used in a fictitious manner. Any resemblance to actual persons, living or dead, or actual events is purely coincidental.

Printed in the United States of America

TABLE OF CONTENTS

The Hidden Manuscript 1
The Enigmatic Symbols 5
The Potion Master's Riddle 7
The Elemental Elixirs 11
The Alchemist's Apprentice 15
The Philosopher's Stone 19
The Legacy Unveiled 23

THE HIDDEN MANUSCRIPT

In the heart of Eldoria, a quaint town cradled between ancient hills and winding cobblestone streets, lay the Eldorian Archive—a forgotten library rich with history. Emily, a young and inquisitive scholar, often sought solace among its dusty tomes and neglected scrolls, immersing herself in the embrace of forgotten knowledge.

One gloomy afternoon, while exploring the dimly lit shelves, Emily's fingers brushed against the spine of an unusually old and worn manuscript. The cover bore no title, only intricate, faded patterns hinting at a storied past. Intrigued, she pulled the aged book from its resting place and blew away the dust that clung to its pages.

As Emily carefully turned the delicate parchment, her eyes widened at the sight of alchemical symbols and mysterious diagrams. The manuscript was a treasure trove of forgotten wisdom, revealing the existence of an ancient alchemist's legacy—an untold story waiting to be uncovered.

Her curiosity ignited, Emily began translating the cryptic text with nimble fingers, unveiling a tale of an alchemist whose name had been erased by time. The manuscript hinted at potions capable of bending reality and elixirs with the power to reveal secrets hidden from mortal eyes.

This discovery sparked a yearning within Emily—a desire for adventure and the pursuit of knowledge that transcended the ordinary. Little did she know that the hidden manuscript would become the key to unlocking a world of magic, mystery, and the alchemical legacy long dormant in the shadows of Eldoria.

Guided by the revelations within the hidden manuscript, Emily's journey led her to an old alchemist's workshop on the outskirts of Eldoria. Nestled in a grove of ancient oak trees, the workshop exuded an aura of forgotten magic.

Upon entering, the air seemed to shimmer with the lingering essence of centuries-old alchemical experiments.

The workshop was filled with glass vials, distillation apparatus, and mysterious ingredients neatly arranged on dusty shelves. A large wooden desk in the center caught her eye, bearing an open journal covered in the same enigmatic symbols found in the hidden manuscript.

Driven by her scholarly passion, Emily meticulously translated the symbols. Each stroke of her quill unraveled a layer of the alchemist's wisdom. The symbols spoke of potions that could heal, reveal truths hidden in shadows, and forge connections between the mundane and the magical.

Among the faded ink and parchment, Emily discovered a set of symbols that seemed to glow with a subtle luminescence. Intrigued, she followed their guidance, unlocking the secrets of elemental elixirs—potions attuned to the primal forces of fire, water, air, and earth.

As Emily brewed her first elemental elixir—a potion that harnessed the essence of fire—the workshop flickered with a warm, mystical glow. The flames in the hearth danced with newfound vitality, and a gentle breeze seemed to whisper secrets from ages long past.

Emily's understanding of the alchemist's legacy deepened. The enigmatic symbols became a bridge between her world and the ancient art of alchemy. With each potion brewed, she felt a connection to the long-vanished alchemist, their knowledge now pulsating through her veins. Her journey had only just begun, and the workshop promised to unveil even more profound mysteries as she delved further into Eldoria's magical history.

THE ENIGMATIC SYMBOLS

Guided by the revelations within the hidden manuscript, Emily's journey led her to an old alchemist's workshop on the outskirts of Eldoria. Nestled in a grove of ancient oak trees, the workshop exuded an aura of forgotten magic.

Upon entering, the air seemed to shimmer with the lingering essence of centuries-old alchemical experiments. The workshop was filled with glass vials, distillation apparatus, and mysterious ingredients neatly arranged on dusty shelves. A large wooden desk in the center caught her eye, bearing an open journal covered in the same enigmatic symbols found in the hidden manuscript.

Driven by her scholarly passion, Emily meticulously translated the symbols. Each stroke of her quill unraveled a layer of the alchemist's wisdom. The symbols spoke of potions that could heal, reveal truths hidden in shadows, and forge connections between the mundane and the magical.

Among the faded ink and parchment, Emily discovered a set of symbols that seemed to glow with a subtle luminescence. Intrigued, she followed their guidance, unlocking the secrets of elemental elixirs—potions attuned to the primal forces of fire, water, air, and earth.

As Emily brewed her first elemental elixir—a potion that harnessed the essence of fire—the workshop flickered with a warm, mystical glow. The flames in the hearth danced with newfound vitality, and a gentle breeze seemed to whisper secrets from ages long past.

Emily's understanding of the alchemist's legacy deepened. The enigmatic symbols became a bridge between her world and the ancient art of alchemy. With each potion brewed, she felt a connection to the long-vanished alchemist, their knowledge now pulsating through her veins. Her journey had only just begun, and the workshop promised to unveil even more profound mysteries as she delved further into Eldoria's magical history.

THE POTION MASTER'S RIDDLE

Armed with newfound knowledge and the glow of elemental elixirs, Emily's quest led her to the mystical forest outskirts of Eldoria, where rumors spoke of a reclusive potion master. Legend had it that this master guarded the next level of alchemical secrets and could only be found by those who solved a series of intricate riddles.

Guided by the symbols and wisdom from the hidden manuscript, Emily ventured deep into the forest, where ancient trees stood sentinel, their twisted branches forming natural archways leading to the potion master's hidden lair.

As Emily approached the entrance, a spectral voice echoed through the trees, presenting her with a riddle that challenged her intellect and understanding of the mystical arts. Each correct answer brought her one step closer to the elusive potion master.

Through moonlit glades and under the canopy of ancient oaks, Emily deciphered the riddles, unveiling the secrets of the forest and the interconnectedness of nature's magic. At the heart of the labyrinthine woods, she discovered the potion master's sanctum—a hidden grove bathed in the soft glow of luminescent flora.

The potion master, draped in robes adorned with alchemical symbols, emerged from the shadows. A silent understanding passed between them, and the potion master presented Emily with a vial containing a shimmering liquid—a concoction that held the essence of the forest itself.

Emily's encounter with the potion master marked a turning point in her journey. The riddles became a gateway to deeper realms of alchemical wisdom, and the forest, with its mystical guardian, offered a glimpse into the symbiotic relationship between the natural world and the ancient art of potion-making.

THE ELEMENTAL ELIXIRS

With the potion master's blessing, Emily delved further into the alchemist's legacy, guided by the luminescent vial containing the essence of the forest. The journey led her to an ancient laboratory hidden within Eldoria's mystical enclave, where she discovered an array of rare ingredients that seemed to hum with latent magic.

The laboratory, bathed in the soft glow of enchanted crystals, held clues to the creation of elemental elixirs beyond those she had previously encountered. As Emily pored over ancient tomes and deciphered inscriptions on the laboratory walls, she unraveled the mysteries of elixirs attuned to water, air, and earth.

In her meticulous experimentation, Emily discovered that each elemental elixir resonated with a specific aspect of the natural world. The elixir of water, when brewed correctly, revealed visions of distant lands and whispered secrets carried by the ocean's currents. The elixir of air granted her the ability to perceive the unseen and heightened her senses to the ethereal energies that surrounded her. The elixir of earth connected her to the very heartbeat of the land, enhancing her resilience and grounding her in the present.

Guided by the luminescent vial, Emily's brewing skills reached new heights. The laboratory became a symphony of alchemical arts, as her experiments harmonized with the ancient wisdom contained within the enchanted forest's essence.

As the elemental elixirs infused her being with their magic, Emily felt a profound connection to the natural world. The laboratory, once a silent witness to centuries of alchemical endeavors, now pulsed with renewed vitality, echoing the dance between the alchemist's legacy and the elemental forces that shaped Eldoria.

Emily's mastery of elemental elixirs became a testament to her growing expertise. The laboratory, with its mystical ambiance, became a sacred space where the past and present converged, and Emily, attuned to the elements, prepared to face the challenges that lay ahead in her pursuit of the alchemist's legacy.

THE ALCHEMIST'S APPRENTICE

Buoyed by her success with the elemental elixirs, Emily's journey through Eldoria took an unexpected turn as rumors of her alchemical prowess reached the ears of a mysterious figure—the long-lost apprentice of the alchemist whose legacy she sought.

One evening, as Emily perused her notes in the enchanting glow of the laboratory, a shadowy figure emerged from the folds of the mystical forest. Cloaked in a tattered robe adorned with alchemical symbols, the apprentice revealed herself to be Alyssa, a seeker of knowledge who had traversed realms in search of the one destined to continue their master's work.

Alyssa, with eyes holding the wisdom of ages, recognized Emily's potential as the bearer of the alchemist's legacy. Intrigued by her proficiency in brewing elemental elixirs, Alyssa offered to be Emily's guide, sharing the deeper intricacies of the alchemical arts and the challenges that awaited them.

Together, Emily and Alyssa ventured into Eldoria's hidden corners, uncovering forgotten alchemical enclaves and deciphering ancient scripts detailing the alchemist's experiments with time, space, and reality itself. The apprentice imparted knowledge of astral alchemy—a discipline transcending the boundaries between material and spiritual realms.

As Emily honed her skills under Alyssa's watchful gaze, the mystical forest seemed to respond to their endeavors. Trees whispered secrets, and the air carried echoes of ancient incantations. Emily, now an apprentice in her own right, felt a profound sense of responsibility as she embraced the alchemist's legacy with her newfound mentor's guidance.

The introduction of Alyssa marked a crucial alliance in Emily's quest. The alchemist's apprentice became a companion on the journey, unveiling deeper layers of the alchemical tapestry. Together, Emily and Alyssa faced the challenges of astral alchemy, preparing for revelations that would transcend the boundaries between the seen and unseen in Eldoria's enchanting embrace.

THE PHILOSOPHER'S STONE

As Emily and Alyssa delved deeper into the realms of astral alchemy, the mysteries surrounding the alchemist's legacy took an unforeseen turn. Guided by ancient manuscripts and the whispers of the mystical forest, the duo discovered cryptic references to the most coveted artifact in alchemical lore—the Philosopher's Stone.

The quest for the Philosopher's Stone led them to a hidden chamber deep within Eldoria's heart—a chamber resonating with an otherworldly energy. Illuminated by the soft glow of crystals, the chamber housed a pedestal upon which rested an ornate box bearing symbols that seemed to dance in the ambient light.

With a sense of trepidation and anticipation, Emily and Alyssa opened the box to reveal a radiant gem—the Philosopher's Stone. Its presence filled the chamber with a palpable aura of transformation and possibility. The stone, a culmination of centuries of alchemical wisdom, held the power to transmute base metals into gold and grant immortality.

As Emily held the Philosopher's Stone in her hands, she felt a surge of knowledge and power course through her veins. The stone revealed visions of the alchemist's life, their struggles, and the profound sacrifices made in pursuit of ultimate understanding. The alchemist's legacy was not merely about potions and elixirs, but about the philosophical journey toward enlightenment and the unification of the material and spiritual worlds.

With Alyssa's guidance, Emily learned to harness the stone's power responsibly, understanding that true mastery lay not in wielding its capabilities for personal gain but in using it to further the pursuit of knowledge and harmony.

The discovery of the Philosopher's Stone marked the pinnacle of Emily's journey. The chamber, now a sanctuary of enlightenment, echoed with the timeless wisdom of the alchemist. Emily, holding the legacy of the

Philosopher's Stone, stood at the threshold of a new era—one where the ancient art of alchemy would transcend its boundaries, blending with the wisdom of the ages to illuminate the path forward in the enchanting world of Eldoria.

THE LEGACY UNVEILED

With the Philosopher's Stone in her possession, Emily's journey through the realms of alchemy reached its zenith. The stone's radiant energy illuminated not only her path but also the intricate connections between the alchemical arts and the natural world of Eldoria.

Emily and Alyssa, now bound by their shared pursuit of knowledge, became custodians of the alchemist's legacy. Together, they transformed the ancient laboratory into a haven of enlightenment, where scholars and seekers from far and wide could gather to learn and share their wisdom.

The elixirs and potions that Emily had mastered became tools for healing, exploration, and the unveiling of hidden truths. The forest, once a silent witness to the alchemist's experiments, thrived with renewed vitality, its magic interwoven with the legacy of the Philosopher's Stone.

As the seasons turned, Eldoria blossomed into a center of alchemical wisdom. Emily, with Alyssa by her side, taught aspiring alchemists the delicate balance between the material and spiritual realms. The legacy of the ancient alchemist lived on, not as a mere collection of potions, but as a profound understanding of the interconnectedness of all things.

In the heart of Eldoria, the hidden manuscript, once a forgotten relic, now held a place of honor. Its pages, illuminated by the wisdom of generations, told the story of a young scholar who had embraced the alchemist's legacy and transformed it into a beacon of enlightenment.

Emily's journey had come full circle. The hidden manuscript, the elemental elixirs, the riddles, and the Philosopher's Stone—all had guided her toward a deeper understanding of herself and the world around her. The alchemist's legacy was unveiled, not as an end but as a new beginning—a testament to the enduring power of knowledge, curiosity, and the timeless dance between the seen and unseen in the enchanting world of Eldoria.

What appeared in the 1970s to be an isolated or anomalous explosion has turned out to be a synodical implosion in this third decade of the twenty-first century. This is because of LCMS's commitment to and toleration of the foundational postmodern heresy.

In the pure [truly Lutheran] churches and schools ... God's Word alone should be and remain the only standard and rule of doctrine, to which the writings of no man should be regarded as equal. Everything should be subjected to God's Word...

As we lay down **God's Word—the eternal truth—as the foundation**, we also introduce and quote these writings as a witness of the truth and as the unanimously received, correct understanding of our predecessors who have steadfastly held to the pure doctrine (Formula of Concord).

Postmodernism, the foundational heresy, delenda est.

Anatomy of an Explosion

by Gregory Schulz

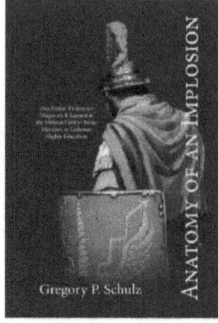

The Woke Marxism taking root in our Lutheran universities is, in fact, a full-scale war against the foundation of Christian churches and schools everywhere. It is a war against the Word incarnate—campaign against the small—l logos of Western civilization as clearly as it is war against the incarnate Logos revealed in the Gospel according to Saint John.

"The truth that Woke Marxists and their academic allies are suppressing is this: although it can be surrendered, language can never be destroyed (Matthew 24:35). Strap on your armor. 'Take and read,' as Augustine writes in Confession." (Preamble).

No less than the heart of the Gospel is at stake. How so? Because the central teaching of Scripture—how sinful man can get right with a holy God—namely, the doctrine of universal justification is the tip of the spear that brings every thought, every teaching, and every agenda captive to the Word, Christ Jesus, the Lord and Savior of the world. The woke Marxist agenda can never be squared with Scripture. Read Anatomy of an Implosion and be enlightened.
Rev. Dr. Mark J. Schreiber CAPT, CHC, USN (Ret.)

This is a must read for anyone concerned about the state of higher Lutheran, Christian, or public education.
The Honorable Nancy Bekx, Wisconsin District VII Reserve Judge, retired

Anatomy of an Implosion—a book written in the "far louder and more academic" footsteps of Kurt Marquart's 1977 book, Anatomy of an Explosion—is an adaptable blueprint for use in biblical, credal, Christian universities. Above all, this book is a call to arms for individuals of Christian consciences—parents, students, supporters, besieged professors, pastors, and parishioners—for the courage and biblical integrity to repulse the attacks of Woke Marxism in their churches and schools with the Gospel of Jesus the Christ.

Available at www.christiannewsmo.com
$16.95

Anatomy of an Explosion - Missouri in Lutheran Perspective

Concordia Theological Seminary Press, Fort Wayne, Indiana, first published Anatomy of An Explosion - Missouri In Lutheran Perspective by Professor Kurt E. Marquart in 1977. It is a 170-page paperback with some 460 footnotes.

Anatomy of an Explosion is the third number in the Concordia Seminary Monograph Series. Editors David P. Scaer and Douglas Judisch comment: "Anatomy of an Explosion" is an apt title for a monograph describing the conflicting theological forces, which encountered each other in the sixties and seventies of our century. As when black clouds move across a summer sky, the lightning was inevitable.

Available at www.christiannewsmo.com
$11.95

Christian News
48 Issues Per Year

1 Year Subscription - United States - mailed - $45.00

1 Year Subscription - International - mailed - $50.00

1 Year On-line viewing Plus Archives Access - $65.00

Mailed subscriptions include free digital link per current issues

Christian News
684 Luther Lane
New Haven, MO 63068
573-237-3110
news@christiannewsmo.com
www.christiannewsmo.com

www.ingramcontent.com/pod-product-compliance
Lightning Source LLC
LaVergne TN
LVHW010420070526
838199LV00064B/5361